Sidney, Stella, and the Moon

EMMA YARLETT

For
Mum, Dad
and Liz, and
for Alex. With
love always × ×

templar publishing

A Templar Book

First published in the UK
in 2013 by Templar Publishing,
an imprint of The Templar Company Limited,
Deepdene Lodge, Deepdene Avenue,
Dorking, Surrey, RH5 4AT, UK
www.templarco.co.uk

Copyright © 2013 by Emma Yarlett

First edition

ISBN 978-1-84877-943-3

Edited by Libby Hamilton

Printed in China

Sidney, Stella, and the Moon

smash

EMMA YARLETT

Sidney and Stella did
everything together.

FEEDING THE
QUacKs.*

* DUCKS

Stella had a lot of fun with Sidney.

And Sidney had
a lot of fun
with Stella.

But there was one thing that Sidney and Stella did **not** do together.
I wonder what that could be?

Bedtime.

Reading

Oh yes,

Sidney and Stella...

did not...

SHARE.

And this is where our tale begins.

It all started when Sidney would not share his bouncy ball.

It teetered from his fingertips, flew towards the open window...

... and did what bouncy balls do best.

It bounced HIGHER and HIGHER
and HIGHER,

until it was so high it could touch the moo—

SMASH

The moon broke
into a million pieces.

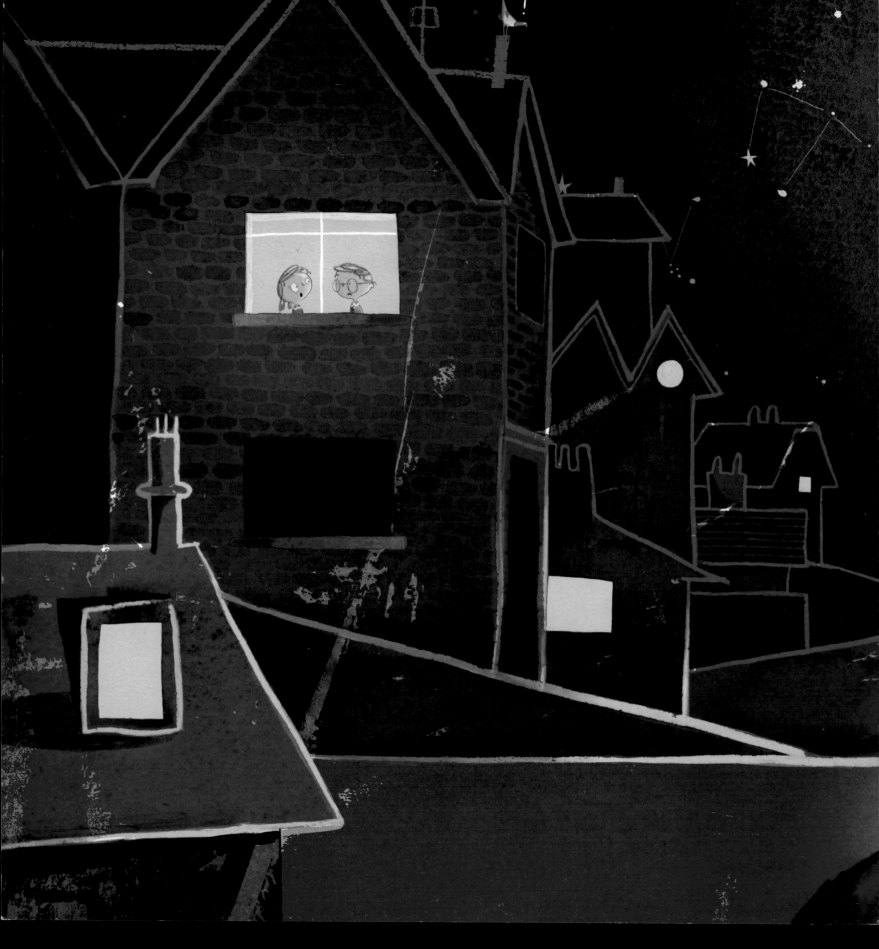

GONE!

Sidney and Stella were **horrified!** There was a big blank space in the night sky. But maybe nobody would notice the moon's sudden disappearance?

Sidney and Stella knew they were in big trouble.

In the morning
they crept downstairs
and slowly opened
their front door...

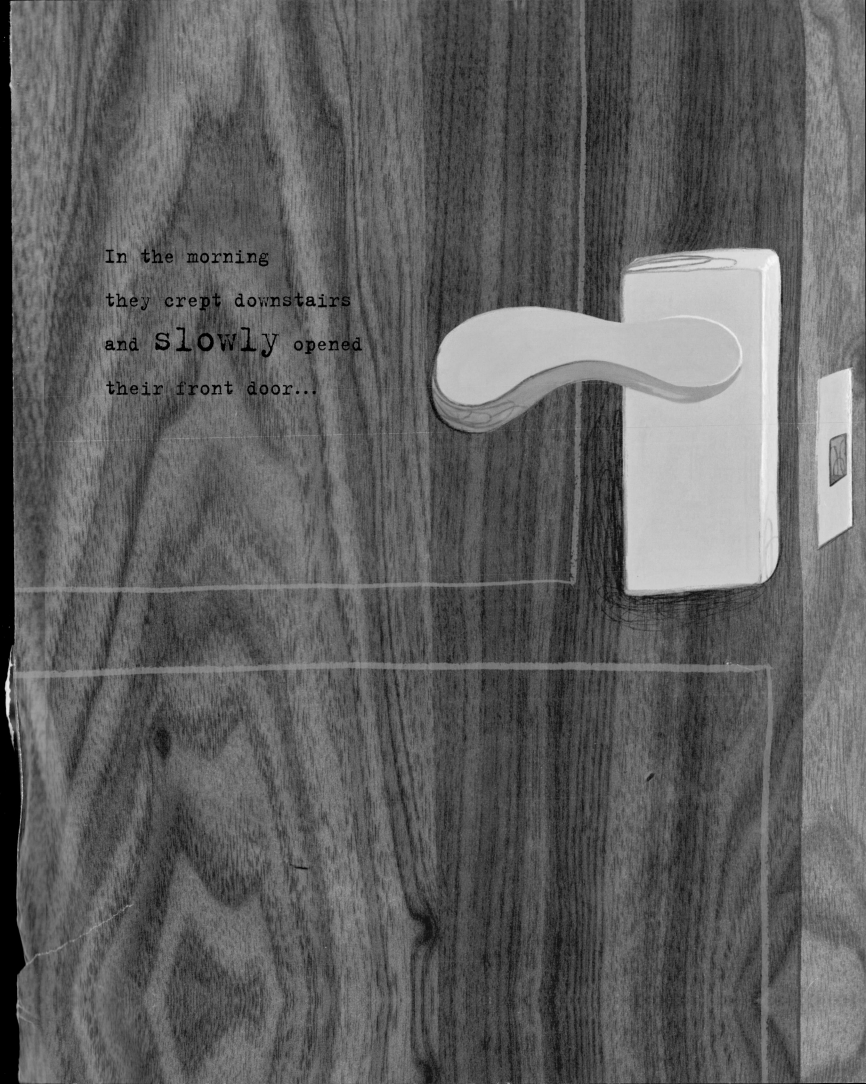

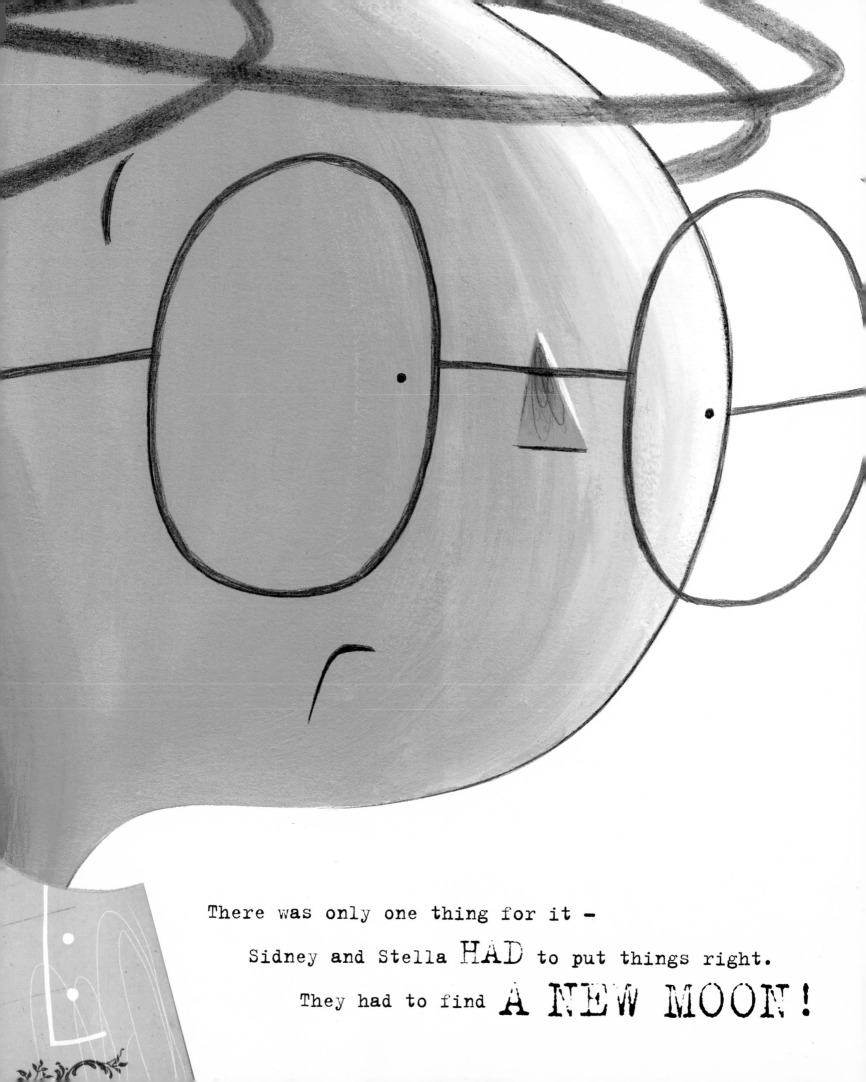

There was only one thing for it –
Sidney and Stella HAD to put things right.
They had to find A NEW MOON!

They searched high...

and low...

but couldn't find **anything**
that could take the place of the moon.

Tired and hungry,

Sidney and Stella took a break.

While Stella tried to think up

a new plan, Sidney decided

to have a cheeky snack...

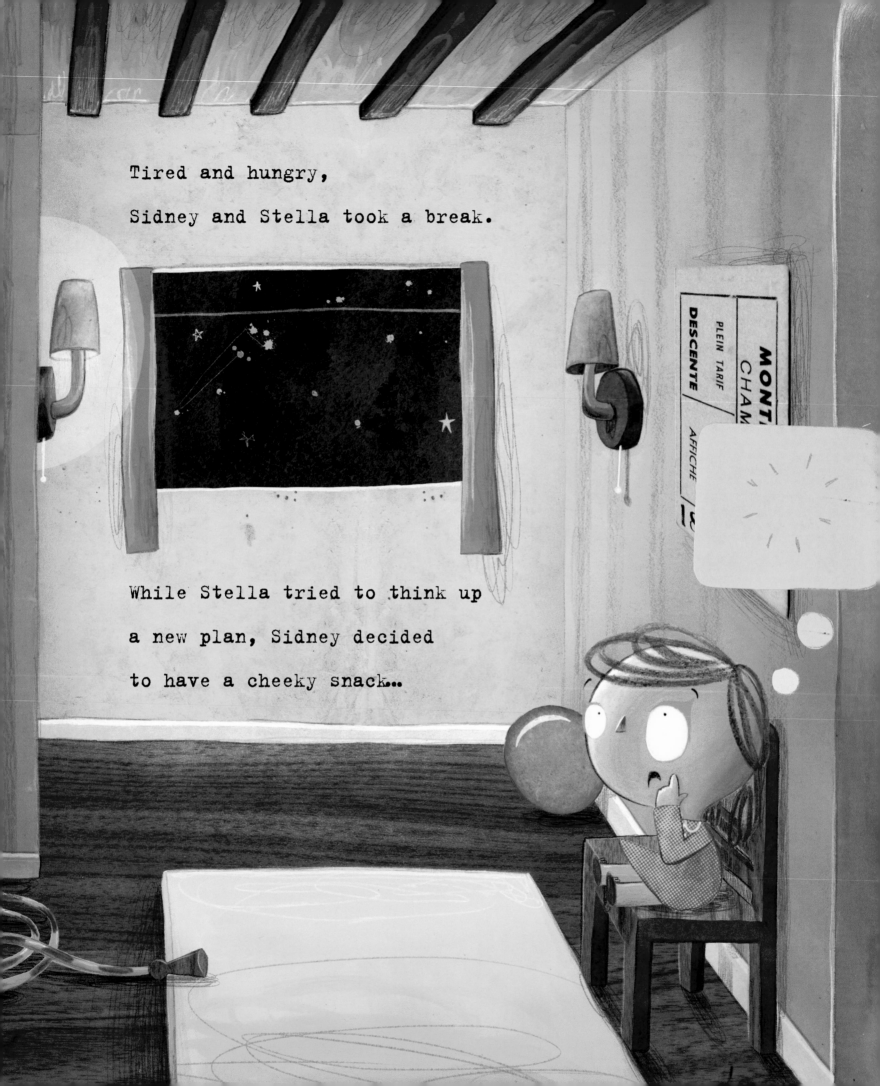

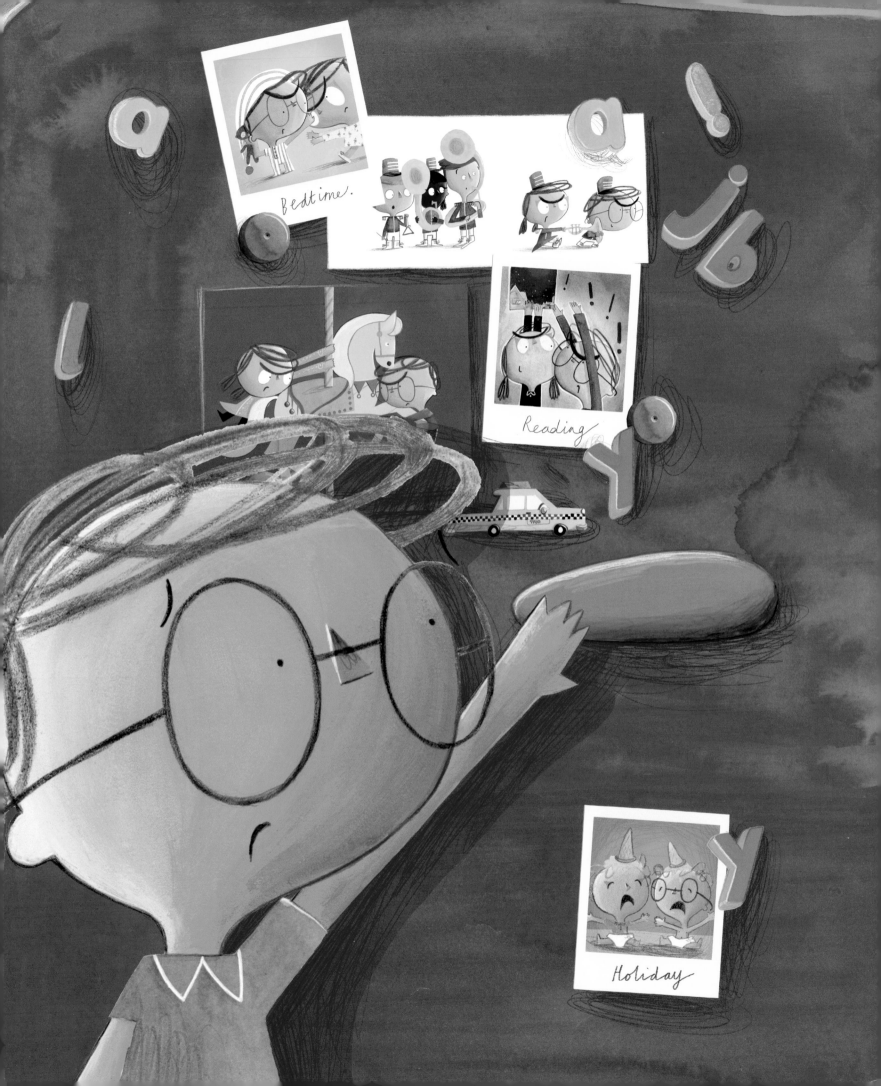

And guess what he found?

And Stella had just the thing to ping
the new moon up into the sky.

But then Sidney and Stella came across an old problem.

I wonder what that could be? Oh yes.

Sidney and Stella...

share?

Sidney and Stella took the new moon and
the skipping rope and rushed outside together.

They set up the catapult...

pulled back the cheese...

and then —

PIING!!..

The 'moon' sat snugly in the night sky once more.

The
END*

* Until Sidney and Stella
share their next adventure...